MW01065048

Tabitha Moon's

HOPPIN'
snake

TATE PUBLISHING & Enterprises

Hoppin' Snake
Copyright © 2010 by Tabitha Moon. All rights reserved.

This title is also available as a Tate Out Loud product. Visit www.tatepublishing.com for more information.

No part of this publication may be reproduced, stored in a retrieval system or transmitted in any way by any means, electronic, mechanical, photocopy, recording or otherwise without the prior permission of the author except as provided by USA copyright law.

The opinions expressed by the author are not necessarily those of Tate Publishing, LLC.

Published by Tate Publishing & Enterprises, LLC
127 E. Trade Center Terrace | Mustang, Oklahoma 73064 USA
1.888.361.9473 | www.tatepublishing.com

Tate Publishing is committed to excellence in the publishing industry. The company reflects the philosophy established by the founders, based on Psalm 68:11,
"The Lord gave the word and great was the company of those who published it."

Book design copyright © 2010 by Tate Publishing, LLC. All rights reserved.
Cover and Interior design by Michael Lee
Illustration by Jason Hutton

Published in the United States of America

ISBN: 978-1-61663-622-7
1. Juvenile Fiction: Animals, General
2. Family & Relationships: Family Relationships
10.06.22

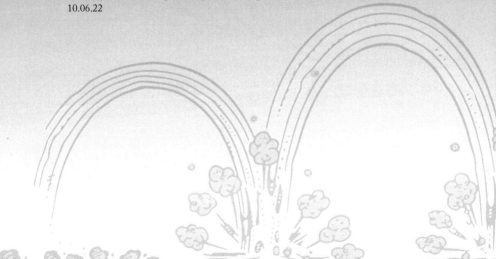

For Gibson,
so that he may always understand
the meaning of family.

Samson Snake didn't know who his parents were. They left Samson all alone in the warm prairie grass of Oklahoma when he was just a baby snake. Rick and Rita Rabbit adopted Samson into their rabbit family. Samson loved the rabbits, and their children, Randy, Rachelle, Riley, and Little Ricky. The rabbits taught Samson how to do many new things, like how to hop and eat carrots, but Samson wanted to find his real family. Late one night, after all of the rabbits had gone to bed, Samson snuck out of the rabbit hole, and went to find his parents.

Samson had traveled all night and found a cool spot to rest under a redbud tree. When he woke up, he began hopping along in search of his family. The sun had begun to heat up the dry grass and Samson was getting hot and thirsty. Samson saw a herd of cows grazing in the field.

"What are you doing out here, and why are you hoppin'?" asked a young calf.

"I am looking for my family. My name is Samson Snake. What is yours?"

"Cory Cow. Why do you hop around?" replied Cory.

"I live with a rabbit family and they taught me to hop," explained Samson. "Which of these cows is your family?"

"Those two brown cows by the pond, but out here it doesn't matter because the whole herd is one big family. We take care of each other," answered Cory.

Cory gave Samson some water to drink and Samson hopped away.

Samson had hopped all day and had passed many different sights along his way. As the sun began to set Samson was thinking about where he would sleep. All of a sudden, Samson saw two bullfrogs hopping beside him.

"Hi!" croaked the two bullfrogs.

"I am Billy, and this is my brother Butch," said one of the bullfrogs.

"My name is Samson Snake. It is nice to meet you two," answered Samson.

"Why aren't you slithering on the ground like other snakes?" asked Butch.

"Yeah, why are you hopping?" asked Billy.

"My family taught me to hop. They are rabbits. I left the rabbit hole to find my real snake family. Do you know my family?" asked Samson.

"No, but our grandpa might," said Butch.

"Yeah, our grandpa is the mayor and he knows everyone," added Billy.

Samson hopped back with the bullfrogs and they introduced him to their grandpa.

"Hello young man. I am Billford B. Bullfrog. How can I help you?" asked Grandpa Bullfrog.

"I am looking for my family. Do you know who they are?" asked Samson.

"Yeah, Grandpa he was raised by rabbits," Butch said.

"Can you believe that?" added Billy.

"Samson, I don't know your family but most snakes like the cooler dirt so they like to stay in the wild prairie grass by the pond. It is on the other side of the big wheat field," Grandpa told Samson. "If you want to stay here with the boys tonight, you can. You will need your rest to go through the big wheat field."

Samson was tired of hopping and wanted to rest so he thanked the bullfrogs, and Butch and Billy showed them where they would sleep.

"Do you like to stay with your grandpa?" asked Samson.

"We live with him," explained Butch.

"He takes care of us instead of our parents," added Billy. The three animals fell quickly asleep.

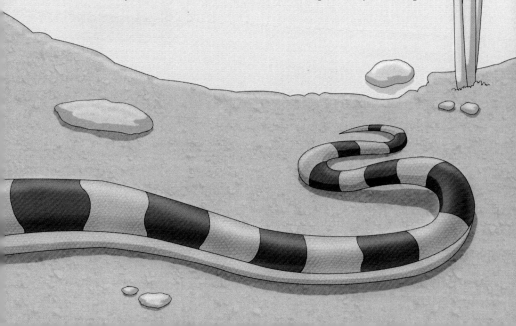

The next day Samson thanked the bullfrogs and began to hop towards the big wheat field. As he was hopping, Samson remembered what Butch and Billy had said about slithering. Samson tried to slither like a snake, but it was a lot of trouble. Samson's tail would pass him or crash into him. He had so much trouble getting his whole body to work together.

An armadillo was passing by and saw Samson. "What are you doing?" asked the armadillo.

"I am trying to slither like a snake," answered Samson.

"Why?" asked the armadillo.

Samson explained to the armadillo that he was on his way to meet his family for the first time. "I don't want them to laugh at me because I can't slither."

The armadillo thought about this for a while and then said, "Why don't you come and eat with my family? You can get some rest from all this slithering."

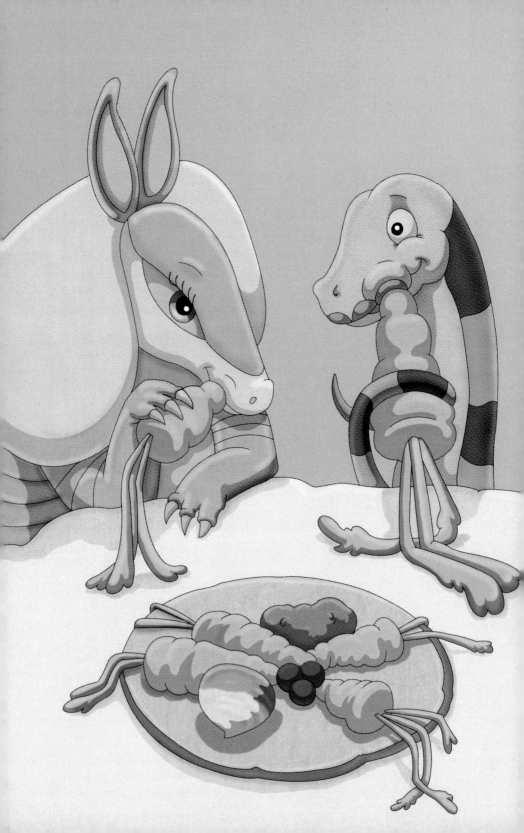

The wheat field was very big and Samson would need to eat so he would have the energy to slither through it.

"Sure," Samson said, exhausted. "What is your name? Mine is Samson."

"Annie," answered the armadillo.

Annie's mom made them lunch and Samson asked about their family. "This is all of our family; it is just my mom and me," said Annie.

Samson didn't know any families with just one parent. "Do you miss your dad?" asked Samson.

"Yes, of course I do. My friends Pete and Patty Prairie Dog help me a lot because they don't have a dad either," answered Annie. "My mom makes me happy, and we do a lot of fun things together. We go to the park, spend time together, and she helps me with my homework. We are just like other families, but different too."

Samson thought about how happy he would be when he met his snake family. Samson thanked the armadillos for lunch and left.

As Samson started to slither through the big wheat field, Farmer Bo picked him up. "Why are you in my big wheat field?" asked Farmer Bo.

Samson told Farmer Bo about the rabbit family and all of the animals he met on the way, and how much he wanted to meet his real family.

"What about the Rabbits?" asked Farmer Bo. "They probably miss you a lot."

Samson had not thought about the Rabbits missing him. It made Samson sad to think about Momma Rabbit crying for Samson. "I love my rabbit family and miss them too." Samson began to cry.

"I will take you back to the rabbit hole," said Farmer Bo.

As Farmer Bo carried him back home, he thought about the different types of families he had met on this trip. Some animals lived with great big families like the cow, some lived with their grandparents like the bullfrogs, some lived with only one parent like the armadillo and the prairie dog, and Samson was adopted by a wonderful family. Farmer Bo laid Samson down by the rabbit hole and Samson hopped inside to hug his family.

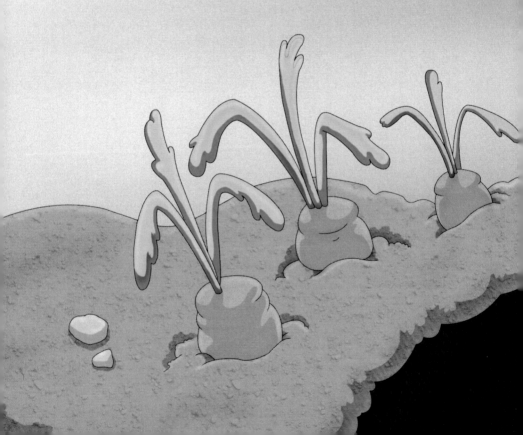

THE end !

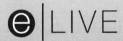

e|LIVE

listen|imagine|view|experience

AUDIO BOOK DOWNLOAD INCLUDED WITH THIS BOOK!

In your hands you hold a complete digital entertainment package. Besides purchasing the paper version of this book, this book includes a free download of the audio version of this book. Simply use the code listed below when visiting our website. Once downloaded to your computer, you can listen to the book through your computer's speakers, burn it to an audio CD or save the file to your portable music device (such as Apple's popular iPod) and listen on the go!

How to get your free audio book digital download:

1. Visit www.tatepublishing.com and click on the e|LIVE logo on the home page.
2. Enter the following coupon code:
   bb40-57dd-bcb4-01cb-a265-7d1e-6bb5-a162
3. Download the audio book from your e|LIVE digital locker and begin enjoying your new digital entertainment package today!